DEAD SHOT

By

C T Mitchell

Copyright

Join My Newsletter

Join my newsletter to win free books, Amazon gift cards, holidays, adventure experiences and much more! Unsubscribe at any time. Go to the end to claim your short read.

TABLE OF CONTENTS

CHAPTER 1

"I'm worried about Nicholas." Pam Weatherby leaned back in her beach chair and closed her eyes behind her over-sized sunglasses. "I know you mean well, darling, by planning a holiday in the middle of the week, but I can't relax when I'm forever thinking of Nicholas. What if he does something while we're away? I'd never forgive myself if something happened and we didn't do anything."

"We are doing something. We're enjoying ourselves on holiday. What else is there to do?" Charles Weatherby tugged the wide brim of his Panama boat hat further down on his forehead. "Nicholas isn't a child, Pam. He's nineteen years old. He's in university. The only thing he should do while we're away is attend class and pass his mid-terms."

"You know that's not what I mean." Pam bit down so hard on her bottom lip that she tasted blood. "What if he has one of his episodes?"

"Why don't you check his YouTube channel? That's the only way any of us can keep track of his comings and goings anymore."

"Brilliant idea!"

She picked up her phone from the white plastic table and tapped on the YouTube app. She knew Nicholas's channel address by heart now. NicSays. They'd watched and re-watched every single video he posted to try to make sense of the dark turn his life had taken since starting college. Pam knew every parent of a troubled child always said, "But he was such a happy boy," and, "We have no idea where this came from," but, in their case, it was true. Nicholas grew up wanting for nothing. Anything he could ever want was just a credit card swipe away. The parade of psychologists they'd taken him to in the last year said it made him entitled and out of touch with reality. He was used to getting what he wanted, and when that didn't happen with the girls he showed interest in, he had the angry teenage boy equivalent of a temper tantrum: he posted nasty things about them online. First it was social media and then he started a YouTube channel with his video blog 'Nic Says.' It turned out Nicholas says a lot of things and none of them were flattering to the girls who refused to date him.

"Maybe you just came on too strong," Pam remembered telling him after he uploaded his first video. "That can happen when you like someone very much. Why don't you try again with a little less demanding and a little more sensitivity? I'm sure that will do the trick."

But it didn't do the trick that time. Or the next time. Or the time after that. It seemed every girl Nicholas approached always had some excuse. They had to study. They had to work. They had a boyfriend. To their credit, they did their best to let him down easy, but it wasn't as easy for Nicholas to put the constant rejection behind him.

“Oh, look, darling, Nicholas’s uploaded a brand new video.”

Pam clicked the play button and held out her phone so they could watch it together. Nicholas's face filled most of the frame. He didn't look dangerous with his shaggy blonde hair and perfect smile. He looked like the sort of boy who would help an old lady cross the street, not mug her and kick her while she was down. He certainly didn't look like the sort of boy anyone would turn down for a date, though Pam admitted to herself that she was more than a little biased on that front. The only thing that seemed even the slightest bit off about Nicholas was his eyes. They shifted back and forth like an over-wound metronome, particularly when he started ruminating on screen.

“Is he on something?” Charles muttered. “He looks as high as a kite.”

“Hush, darling, so we can hear what he has to say.”

“Hi everyone, this is Nicholas. Today on Nic Says is 'payback a bitch – like you lot.' I'd like to dedicate this very special episode to Stephanie, Kate, and Michaela. I tried to be nice. I tried to be rational. I tried to think of all the reasons you might be telling the truth as to why you were too busy to grab a damn cup of coffee or see a movie with me, but I kept coming back to the same conclusion. You're lying. You're lying through your perfectly made up lips, your pearly whitened teeth that Mommy and Daddy paid for, and now it's payback time. You're about to find out that payback is an even bigger bitch than you. See you in Hell, girls."

Nicholas jostled the camera around so he was no longer the focus. Instead, it showed a busy university campus. Nicholas's university, Southern Cross University, Lismore campus. Pam and Charles heard a round of pop-pop-pops that sounded like firecrackers going off. But it wasn't. Amidst the screaming and running and swearing as someone big and burly and dressed all in black tackled Nicholas, they realized their worst fears were fully apparent. Those weren't firecrackers going off. Those were gunshots.

CHAPTER 2

When it came to taking down an offender, Detective Jack Creed was always taught to react first, think later. Judging by the fact that he was the only one who tackled the kid with the sawn off hunting rifle when he started shooting up the campus forequarter, he was the only one that remembered the lesson from police academy.

“I need back up!” he shouted to the campus ground staff, who were standing around with their mouths hanging open. What were they trying to do, catch flies? They better shut their traps and get to helping him out before he beat this squirming, swearing kid into submission himself.

“Just hold him a little while longer, Jack.” Detective Constable Jo Boston-Wright hit the ground like she was sliding into home plate and cuffed the kid. She didn't mind getting down and dirty in the name of the law. That's what Jack liked about her. Jo was the complete opposite of Creed. She could play both sides of the card as needed, rough and tumble cop or undercover first year freshman. Today she was both.

"Boston -Wright to the rescue," he joked.

"As usual" She grinned and brushed her blonde hair out of her face. "I swear campus security is pretty much friggin' useless. You would think they'd be better prepared, especially when you see all that stuff in America with shootings in schools and colleges. But I suppose this is Australia and we are in country town Lismore. Nothing like this has ever happened before."

"Prepared and using your training when it happens are two completely different things." Jack sat up and dragged the offender with him. "I just wish we got here two minutes earlier."

"It is what it is," Jo said.

"Tell that to the families of the girls he shot."

"Who is doing the media spokesperson thing this time? You or me?" She stood and dusted off the knees of her jeans. "'Cause if it's me, I need to put on something that's more we-are-deeply-saddened-and-in-shock instead of I-just-woke-up-after-an-all-night-bender."

"You're the camera-ready one, Jo, not me. Besides, the media prefer a good looking blonde with curves over a wrinkly, grey haired fifty-something-year-old," Jack said with a smirk, knowing full well it would rile up Ms. Hyphenated Surname.

Jo didn't bite. "Why wouldn't they. Not bad for 42.

And you? Fifty? Ha, closer to sixty, I'd say."

Creed shook the offender, who howled for his lawyer. "Good call. Besides, I have this prick to deal with."

"Do we have an official statement yet from Chief Johnston?"

"Not yet. He's probably doing his hair hoping to steal your media career. Just say the usual, 'We are continuing to collect information and process the crime scene. We'll update you when we're able.'"

Boston-Wright grinned again. "Are you sure it should be me and not you addressing the media?"

"I'll flip you for it next time, glamour puss." Jack intimated as he mocked by pouting his lips to look like a chicken's arse. He rattled the offender by the handcuffs. "You're coming with me. There's an interrogation room with your name on it."

*****

"For the last time, I told you I'm not saying anything until you get me a lawyer," Nicholas insisted. "Call my parents if you want. They'll give you the number of the guy we use." Jack burned a hole with his eyes straight through the kid with the private school boy looks, something Jack despised with all his public school heart.

"Oh, you've said plenty already," Jack said. "We've had you on our radar for months. Your videos speak louder than anything you could think to say right here and now."

"What videos?" Nicholas squirmed in the gray plastic chair. "I don't know what you're talking about."

"Don't play dumb with me, sonny," Jack snapped. "You know exactly what videos I'm talking about."

"No, I don't." Nicholas squirmed so hard the chair almost tipped over. "You say I'm the delusional one, but it's not me, it's you."

"Why did you shoot those three girls today?" Jack switched from confrontational to interrogational. Maybe Nicholas would slip up and give away some details for the crime. Maybe not, but trying to catch him off guard or in a 'I'm above the law' delusion was better than nothing. He'd shut up faster than a politician in the middle of a scandal once that lawyer actually showed up. "You had a campus full of people. You could take aim at anyone. Why them?" He slapped three pictures down on the table in front of Nicholas. The three victims. "Why them, huh? Why Stephanie, Kate, and Michaela?"

"Why not?"

"What did they ever do to you?"

He shrugged. "What did they ever not do for me? Plenty. I didn't exist to them. I was a non-person. Now they don't exist either. Don't bother telling me they're just wounded, Detective. I know my aim is impeccable. I've been hunting with my dad since before I could walk. I don't shoot to wound or maim. I shoot to kill."

CHAPTER 3

"How long did you have him going till he clammed up?" Jo stood next to Jack behind the two-way mirror. They could see into the interrogation room but Nicholas couldn't see out. She had come to the police station as soon as the press conference ended. She was still wearing her 'official police spokesperson' blue tailored suit and high heels with her hair pulled back and twisted into a low chignon.

"He can't deny the shooting. He's the one that posted the video online." Jack sipped at his steaming cup of black coffee. "We can stick that on him, maybe more. We're gunning for hate speech. Those videos he posted..." Jack shook his head. He'd seen a lot in his years as a detective, but he never thought one nineteen-year-old kid could have that much hate inside him toward women. He was the sort of kid that made Jack want to hire a bodyguard for his wife and daughter. He couldn't protect those three girls on campus from this monster, what made him think he could protect his own family? "Those videos are our most damning evidence if we can find them."

Jo frowned. “What do you mean if we can find them? They're up on his YouTube page. The guy is obsessed with documenting his every thought and move.”

“Was obsessed with documenting his every thought and move,” Jack corrected. “He's deleted them from his account and the guys in IT can't find a cache. We'll need to get a warrant to search his home to see if we can find the original copies.”

“So he's smarter than he looks, huh?”

“Seems so.” Jack took another long draw from his coffee cup. “His parents are on the way to the station. I think we should separate them and question them to see what they knew while the boys work on getting that warrant approved.”

Jo nodded. “Count me in.”

*****

Charles Weatherby looked up when the door to the tiny interrogation room opened. He pitied any claustrophobic people that might be picked up for questioning. He didn't mind enclosed places and it already felt like the walls were closing in on him.

“Mr. Weatherby, I'm Detective Creed.” Instead of offering to shake his hand, Jack set a folder of crime scene photos in front of Charles. “I'm in charge of your son's case.”

"Do you think my wife or I had anything to do with this event?" Charles asked. "We're just as in shock as anyone else. Nicholas is a good boy." Jack glared back at Charles with a look that showed he had heard it all before.

"Good boys don't shoot up a university campus, do they Mr. Weatherby?"

"He's lost his way." Charles examined his fingers and spun his wedding ring around and around his finger. He looked at anything and everything but the crime scene photos. Jack didn't really blame him. Three families lost their daughters today and his son caused it. Why would he want to be reminded of that? Denial is easier. Denial helps you sleep at night.

"What changes did you notice in your son within the last few months?" Jack asked.

"You mean when he started posting those horrible videos?" Charles looked up and held Jack's gaze for longer than most would. Not bad. He had some guts. Too bad his kid took the coward's way out and took his aggression out on others instead of himself. "Three months ago, Nicholas started changing. He withdrew from us and refused to tell us where he was going or who he was seeing. He dropped all his old friends and only wanted to be alone." Charles frowned. "At least that's what he said. Pam, my wife, and I aren't so sure. We could hear him talking to someone late at night.

More like arguing. They were planning for something, but when we confronted Nicholas about it, he said we were being paranoid and to leave him be. We were forced to subscribe to his YouTube channel if we wanted any hint of what he was up to. He never talked to us anymore. It was like living with a ghost. He was there but not there. Pam and I are just as shocked as anyone else by today's events on campus. Believe me, Detective Creed, if we could have stopped it, we would have."

"When you say you heard him arguing with someone at night, did you ever question him about it?"

"We tried, but he always got upset and told us to mind our own business and stay out of his life." Charles spread his hand out in front of him in a hopeless, helpless gesture. "That's when we subscribed to his YouTube channel. Why would he tell the world what he was thinking but not his own parents? We didn't understand, though we wanted to. We took him to the best specialists money could buy, but he shut everyone out. He shut us out most of all."

"Could you hear this other person at all? Did Nicholas ever talk to them over Skype or some other video call program?"

Charles shook his head. "He could have been arguing with himself for all we know. With how his health was recently, I wouldn't doubt it. He's very fragile emotionally and mentally, Detective Creed. We sheltered him from the harshness of people and the world at large, but I think what we saw as a service actually was a disservice. He couldn't cope and now those poor girls and their families are suffering because of it."

"We're going to need to search your house," Jack said. "It's probably best if you're not there. With the media crawling around, you're going to thank us for that advice later."

Charles nodded. "I understand. We were on holiday. We can just go back up there. I can leave our cell number in case you need us for anything. Do you have children, Detective Creed?"

Jack sipped at his rapidly cooling coffee. "Two. My son lives in Sydney. He's an architect. And my daughter, she's at uni. She and her mother live in Brisbane. Better medical care up there. I see them when I can, which is mostly on weekends."

"If your daughter did something so horrible and so heinous that you couldn't wrap your head around it, what would you do?"

"I'd do the same thing you and your wife are doing," Jack assured him. "Sometimes people are just broken, but no matter how hard we try to fix them, it's really up to them to fix themselves." Jack looked at Charles with understanding.

CHAPTER 4

The Weatherby house was eerily quiet. Jack and Jo led the team to Nicholas's basement bedroom. "Dust for prints," Jack ordered. "Based on interviews with his parents, we might be looking for a second person as well."

"Just what we need. Two women haters running loose." Jo crouched down and shined a flashlight under the bed. "This guy should have just accepted that no means no and moved on. Instead, he goes out and kills three girls."

"Maybe it's not that they said no but how they said it," Constable Jenkins, one of the cops dusting for prints, said. "I mean, what makes ladies so above the law? You lot walk around thinking your shit don't stink and we're supposed to be okay when you push us aside without any valid reason?"

"Oh, don't even tell me you're standing up for the little punk!" Jo pulled several boxes out from under the bed. "He asked the girls to coffee, and they said no. That should be the end of the discussion. He could have found someone that said yes eventually. There's always someone desperate enough to date emotional cripples, especially if they're loaded like this kid is."

"So you think he should have flashed his trust fund when he asked the girls out?" Jenkins argued. "Would that have changed their answers? Would that have saved their lives?"

Boston-Wright shrugged. "Maybe, but we'll never know now, will we? There's no point arguing about it and there's definitely no point in you sticking up for the creep."

"If that were us – if I walked up to you and asked you to coffee – what would you say, Jo?" Constable Jenkins asked. "And be honest. If you're all about a woman's right to choose and not be afraid to speak her mind, you'll be honest and not try to let me down easy."

"See, if you go into it thinking I'm going to shoot you down, what's the point?" she asked. "You're doing the same thing this Nicholas kid did. You're going in expecting the worst and, when it happens, you blame the victim. No one likes to be harassed. I doubt he just asked any of these girls out for coffee once and was done with it. No, this has all the hallmarks of obsession. He was obsessed with tearing down these girls, maybe all girls on campus, and this is the result."

"So how about that cup of coffee, Jo?"

"In your dreams, Constable."

"Let's just get what we came for," Jack warned. "Jo, can you turn on Nicholas's laptop? Perfect. Leave it to the kid to not password protect his stuff. Didn't he think he was going to get to caught?"

"They never do," Jo said. "It's the entitlement factor, remember?"

"Well, our entitled mass murderer left quite the video trail." Jo double clicked on the video with the earliest created on date. Nicholas's face instantly popped up on screen.

"Hi all. This is Nicholas and you're watching Nic Says. I know a lot of you are going to say 'so what's up with all this whining? Just suck it up and move on, dude,' but I can't. How would you feel if your heart got ripped out and stomped on by someone you used to think was so nice? Steph, this is for you. You acted so nice in chemistry class, but the second I make a move and ask you out, you turn into a total bitch. What gives? How can you lead someone on like that? I thought you liked me. You acted like you did. I guess you were just playing games. I don't like being toyed with. I'm not something to bat around and discard when you're bored or when things aren't going your way. Do you like being in control? Well, guess what? You can't always be in control. I'm in control and you're going to get what's coming to you. You heard it here first, Steph. You're going to get what's coming to you. Either you die or I die, and it's not going to be me."

“And that's why we've been trailing the kid for months,” Jack said. Jo clicked on the next video. Nicholas's face filled the screen again.

“Hi all. This is Nicholas from Nic Says. Today's video is dedicated to Kate. I bet you thought I'd still be crying over Stephanie, right? Wrong. Steph is not worth my time and I definitely didn't cry over her. She's just a bitch like all her friends in that damn women's studies class that I took to try to understand you bitches better. That's right. I thought I could learn a thing or two, but it turns out it's just a bunch of stuck up femnazis that want to bash men and then cry about gender inequality. Here's an idea. Stop being the double standard. You can't cry about being underrepresented or whatever and then turn around and make me feel like shit in class ‘cause I dared challenge your view or perspective. That's why we have debates, dumbass. There are two sides to every story, and this is mine. Kate, you think you're all high and mighty and would rather – and I quote – 'drink antifreeze' than date me? Well, here's a little tip for you. Death is pain. I'm going to make sure you feel as much terror and fear as I felt when you and your minions jumped all over my shit in class. You may lord over them, but you're not going to lord over me. Payback is a bitch and you'll get what's coming to you.”

“Jesus, that kid is troubled.” Jo combed through the box she pulled from under the bed. It was like a treasure chest of anti-feminism literature. “Why take a women's studies class if you hate women?"

"I don't think he started out hating women." Jack clicked on the next video. "I think what he saw as the constant rejection and hypocrisy pushed him over the edge."

"Not everyone goes to that extreme when they're pushed over the edge," Jo reminded Jack.

"Not everyone is Nicholas Weatherby."

"Yeah, thankfully."

Nicholas's face filled the screen again. "Hi all. This is Nicholas from Nic Says. Today's video blog is brought to you courtesy of Michaela. Michaela, you need no introduction, but I'll set the scene anyway. Remember when you asked me to be your study partner? Remember when you set up all those late night meetings in the library and coffee shop? You said it was just for school, but why did you call and text so much if you were just interested in school related things? I thought there was more, but you thought you could just use me for a male perspective on the project and then drop me faster than your pants at a frat party. But whatever. I didn't judge. I thought it was a one-time deal and that you were still a good person. How wrong I was. You, Michaela, proved time and time again the meaning of the word tease. I hope you're happy with your behavior. I'm the last guy you'll ever treat with such disrespect."

"Those are the big ones," Jack said. "We can use the other video blog entries to show a pattern of how he felt repeatedly disrespected and led on by these girls until he took matters into his own crazy hands."

"What about phone, text, and instant messenger records?" Jo asked. "I know we'll have to put in a request for the phone and text message records, but what about IM? Did he save any of those logs on his computer?"

Jo searched through all the files and folders till she found what they were hoping for. "Bingo. Let's see who Nicholas was talking to leading up to the crime."

CHAPTER 5

Jack crowded close to read the chat transcript over Jo's shoulder. It started out innocently enough. Nicholas, under the internet handle Nsez, was talking to someone who went by the handle BigGuns. They exchanged, "Hey, how are you," and, "Good, man, you?" before it delved into more sinister territory.

Nsez: Did you get the guns?
BigGuns: I always get the guns. It's easy when you know where to look and I know where to look.
Nsez: We can't keep them here. I can't have anyone get suspicious that I'm planning more than just an internet rant.
BigGuns: I know a place. You can pick it up on your way to campus.
Nsez: Me? I thought we were in this together.
BigGuns: We are, but if someone tips the cops off, we need to be able to finish the job. We can't go in together. Those bitches have probably already blabbed to campus security about how 'threatened' you make them feel. The cops will be expecting you to do something. They won't think twice about me.

Nsez: So I go in first and then you follow?
BigGuns: Not the same day.
Nsez: But what's the point if we don't take care of all the bitches at once? We need to hit them while everyone is scared. There's more confusion that way. You'll be able to blend with the crowd.
BigGuns: What we need is to keep the element of fear. If they know you didn't act alone, the bitches will be freaked morning, noon and night. That's payback till we bring the curtain down on the final act with a BANG.
Nsez: No one will overlook me ever again.
BigGuns: Trust me, you'll be legendary.
Nsez: So, same time/place as we talked about?
BigGuns: Definitely. See you there.

"The parents were right." Jack set his mouth in a firm, grim line that most people just called his 'regular expression.' "We're dealing with two offenders here. Constable Jenkins, call the university and let them know to be on high alert. Get a copy of his cell phone records while you're at it. See if he's called or texted anyone more than usual. Check for patterns. Jo, read through these chat transcripts and look for any clues as to BigGuns' identity. Call me if you find anything. I'm going to campus to see if our second suspect is as cocky as our first."

"Got it." Jo turned her attention back to the chat transcript.

Nsez: Man, I am so tired of those bitches always thinking they're so above everyone else. Women's studies? It should be called Male Bashing 101. That would be more accurate.
BigGuns: Tell me about it. If that's how they talk when we are around, think about what they say when we're not there. I bet they all hang out together and bash, bash, bash nonstop.
Nsez: They deserve what's coming to them.
BigGuns: Payback's a bitch.
Nsez: lol. Just like them.

Were they planning to take down the entire women's studies class? Jo skimmed the transcript looking for answers. She had a horrible feeling they were running out of time. "Come on, Jack. You stopped one offender; I need to find you enough info to do it again."

Nsez: The professor should have called today's lesson 'Gang up on Nicholas.' I say one little thing against their idea of what's 'right' and 'fair' and they jump all over my shit.
BigGuns: Dumb bitches don't know they are marked. They'd be nicer if they knew not to mess with you. Pretty soon everyone will know not to mess with you.
Nsez: Damn straight. Sometimes I want to tell them what's coming just to see their reaction. I want to see the fear. I want to look them in the eye and tell them they're going to die.

BigGuns: The less you say the better. We need to keep everyone guessing.
Nsez: I'm tired of waiting.
BigGuns: Not long now. Pretty soon everyone will know your name.
Nsez: And the bitches will be dead.
BigGuns: Bang, bang, bang.

Clearly, the second suspect shared Nicholas's opinions and goaded him on just as much – if not more – than the girls in class. But who were they? Jo needed to find more clues before it was too late.

Nsez: So you know a lot about me, but you've never really told me much about you. We leave things at the drop location but are never there at the same time. What gives?
BigGuns: It's not a good idea if we're seen together. It's better this way.
Nsez: But how can we plan if I don't know anything about you?
BigGuns: You know plenty about me. You just don't need to know everything.
Nsez: Is this a setup? Are you going to get me to do your dirty work and then back out?
BigGuns: Of course not.
Nsez: Then tell me who you are.
BigGuns: You know who I am.
Nsez: No, I don't! If I did, I wouldn't be asking.

BigGuns: You know who I am. We're in class together.
Nsez: Women's studies?
BigGuns: Bingo. I hate those bitches just as much as you do. They deserve to know as much fear and terror as we can squeeze out of them. Don't back out on me now, Nicholas. We need to see this through.
Nsez: From here, it looks like you plan for me to take the fall and you to walk away with no one knowing any differently.
BigGuns: That's not true. Watch the TV screens. I'll be up there with you before long.
Nsez: Are you sure?
BigGuns: Positive. Now, do you remember the drop location?
Nsez: The storm drain next to the campus cafe.
BigGuns: Bingo. What you need will be waiting for you there.
Nsez: What about you?
BigGuns: I'll be ready for round two on Friday. Two 'events' in one week. Those bitches won't know what hit them.
Nsez: Make sure you follow through, okay? I don't want to take the fall.
BigGuns: I'll show you mine if you show me yours. ;)
Nsez: Just promise you'll go through with it.
BigGuns: You first.
Nsez: I promise.
BigGuns: Me too.

Nsez: Say you promise. Say the words.
BigGuns: I promise.

"Jenkins, any luck with those phone and text message logs?" Jo called.

"No good," the Constable said. "His cell phone company sent me e-copies of the records and there's no pattern. He didn't talk to anyone that stands out as suspicious. It must all be online."

"That's what I was afraid of." Jo punched Jack's number into her cell phone. "Jack, are you at the university yet?"

"Just got here."

"Good. The drop location is in the storm drain by the campus cafe. Check if our second suspect left anything incriminating. The only other clues we've been able to find is that they're in the women's studies class with each other and that's the big finale – taking out everyone in class."

"I'll check the class roster and see if anyone has been missing class since the incident," Jack promised. "You'll be giving a lot more media briefings after this, Ms Boston-Wright."

She laughed humorlessly. "Let's just hope it's for the right reason."

"Send back up, just in case."

"I'm on my way now."

CHAPTER 6

Jack found the storm drain near campus cafe and jumped down into the dry runoff area. Someone had removed the metal grate over the tunnel; the better to hide things inside. Jack snapped on his flashlight and crept inside.

"Jesus," he muttered when his flashlight illuminated hate speech graffiti all over the walls.

Kill the bitches!
The only good girl is a dead girl.
Shotgun says...dead!
Kiss kiss bang bang.
No means no, and dead means dead.

He needed to check that class roster list and he needed to check it now.

*****

"You know, I know a lot of people will say differently, but I actually feel safer since the incident on campus." The clerk in the registrar office chatted amiably as Jack waited for her to print out a copy of the Women's

Study class roster. “The constant police presence and media attention is rather comforting.”

“Glad someone feels that way.” Jack made a 'wrap it up' motion with his hand. “I really need that list of names, so if you can hurry it up, I'd appreciate it. Also, crosscheck it with any absences since Wednesday.”

“That's not my job. You'll have to check with the professor that teaches the course if you want class attendance.”

“I'll be sure to do that.”

The clerk handed over the class roster. “There you go. Hot off the press.”

Jack looked down at the list. Nicholas was one of only five guys in the class. He'd bet big money that BigGuns was one of those guys. Should he find them or go talk to the professor about attendance? There was no time to track down five guys with the clock ticking on another attack. He needed to go straight to the source: the Professor.

Professor Jennifer Whitman’s office was in the second floor of the humanities building. Jack walked there as quickly as he could without looking panicked or suspicious. As far as anyone knew, he was just a guy in a dark suit, not a cop, not press, and not anyone to concern themselves with. If the suspect knew they were on to him, would that bump the crime up? Would he aim to take out the cops instead of the girls in class? Or would something else entirely go down if he couldn't get there in time? Jack didn't want to even think about how many people were on campus. They were all in danger. No one was safe.

Jack took the stairs two at a time. Class was set to begin in ten minutes. He hoped he could still catch Professor Whitman in her office. "Professor?" Jack knocked once on the door.

"Detective Jack Creed, Kingscliff Police Department. I need to speak to you." He waited for an answer. When none came, he opened the door himself. The office was empty. But the dry erase boards were not. Scrawled in red marker wherever there was space were the same words from the storm drain:

Kill the bitches!
The only good girl is a dead girl.
Shotgun says...dead!
Kiss kiss bang bang.
No means no, and dead means dead.

Their second suspect wasn't another angry male. It was an angry female. Their second suspect is Professor Jennifer Whitman.

CHAPTER 7

Jack didn't give himself time to think. He just ran. He ran down the stairs to the first floor where the women's study class was held.

"Please don't let me be too late. Please don't let me be too late," he chanted under his breath. As he ran, he pulled his gun out of the holster hidden under his jacket. He was going to need it. It could be the difference between one casualty and thirty-five.

As Jack neared the door, he could see Professor Whitman through the window of the classroom door. She was standing in front of class smiling as if it were just any other regular day. Her words filtered out into the hallway.

"Class, I know you've been spooked by the events that happened Wednesday. Three of our own are no longer with us and one is locked up. It's a true tragedy. I am truly shocked that no one put the pieces together and followed the trail to Nicholas sooner. That boy was crying out for attention and no one heard. What's even more of a tragedy is that no one will hear you either. No one will hear your screams before it's too late. You call yourself feminists. You say you are interested in gender equality, but you're just spoiled children, playing at an ideal that used to stand for something. It used to mean more than just debating in a classroom. It used to mean taking the ideas out into the world and doing something about it. The world has grown soft. You have grown soft. I refuse to watch all my life's hard work, blood, sweat, and tears be destroyed by a classroom full of wannabes. I always wanted to be remembered and now no one will ever forget my name."

Jack kicked in the door and fired three shots at Professor Whitman in the front of the room just as she was pulling a semi-automatic Beretta 92 FS from her messenger bag. Blood splattered the white dry erase board. Professor Whitman looked down as her white shirt rapidly turned red with blood.

The classroom was swarming with campus staffers and local Lismore police before Jack had time to even lower his gun. "Detective Jack Creed." He flashed his badge. "The threat is contained."

*****

"So what's the latest?" Jack asked as Jo approached. She was dressed in her press conference clothes again. That blue power suit was going to get quite the workout in the coming weeks.

"She'll live. . .barely. The good news is you saved that classroom full of students. We're executing a search warrant of her apartment now. Professor Whitman seems too full of herself to not keep some sort of manifesto detailing all her thoughts and opinions. We'll get her. There are too many witnesses that can pin her as the mastermind of this whole situation."

"Good work, Jo." Jack sipped at his coffee. "We make a good team. Your media skills and my good old fashion policing." Jack chuffed. Jo smiled and moderately nodded, not wanting to show Jack too much that she agreed with him.

"Well, until next time," Jack quipped as he started out the door. "Perhaps you ought to think about a sea change, Jo? Kingscliff is Heaven on Earth, you know." Jo smiled.

BONUS CHAPTER

Thank you for reading *Dead Shot*. As a bonus, I have included a chapter of Dead Boss, the novella that went #1 in category on Amazon US & UK. I hope you enjoy it.

Dead Boss (previously published as Murder on the Beach)

Detective Jack Creed leaned against the kitchen cupboards looking across his lounge through the beach gums to the ocean. His hands rested on the granite bench top, fingers pursed as if he were beginning the Olympic 100 meter dash.

It was an autumn Sunday morning, one of Jack's favourite times of the year. The air was crisp and the crystal clear ocean waves pounded onto the beach. Jack was in a moment of contemplation. It had been three years since he had moved from Brisbane and taken up residency at the Seaview Motel at Cabarita Beach. The double standards of the Brisbane C I D did not sit well with Jack's morals, a copper who played the game straight down the middle. Let's say the move over the border was mutual. Jack didn't have any time for Chief Constable O'Halloran and his Fortitude Valley 'dining mates' of Italian extraction and O'Halloran didn't like Jack's unorthodox ways.

The Seaview Motel commanded an absolute ocean front position in Cabarita Beach; the only one on the strip. Built in the early '70s, what the place lacked in modern facilities, it certainly made up for in charm. Robin looks after the reservations at the motel and all things administrative. Now on the wrong side of 65, she would have been quite a looker in her day. William, her husband, who fancied himself as a Robert Gourlet lookalike and used the line on all the females staying at the motel, looked after the pool and the motel's well-manicured, landscaped gardens. The gardens really added to the character of the place. None of this modern, sparse landscape featuring Australian naturals. Instead, the golden cane palms shaded the guests by the pool reached by walking across blue cooch lawn. It felt so good walking across this carpet of velvet; it reminded Jack of growing up in North Queensland as a young boy playing football and tackling his mates Peter Gill and Karl Tinus to the ground. It was always a soft landing, something you now can't experience by walking over pebble blasted concrete on your way to a 5-star resort pool at the Sofitel.

Robin was a charming host, often calling her guests 'darling' while William gave his classic Robert Gourlet pose fantasizing that he looked as good as the movie star. They ran a great business here for some offshore mining guy who visits once in a while.

Robin and William liked having Jack around the motel. He gave the place a sense of security. Although the town was a fairly quiet place, occasionally a bit of riffraff from Brisbane would venture down and cause a little bit of mayhem after a few sherbets. The motel was a favourite for wedding guests, often hosting ceremonies in the gardens or on the front grassy path with stunning ocean vistas. It made for a perfect backdrop in a couple's life long memories of their splendid day. Once Jack had to step in between a father and his new son-in-law after both had too much jungle juice on the wedding night, but that was as rowdy as it got.

But for Jack, Cabarita Beach was sometimes not a secure place for him. His family, including his troubled daughter, lived in Brisbane because the city housed better medical facilities. Melissa had been battling depression for five years now and there seemed no answer in sight. Jack missed his family and would do anything for them. And this meant working longer and farther away from the ones he loved so much. But Jack was lucky. He was away from O'Halloran and doing a job he loved.

Jack sipped on his black coffee. Today it was instant but normally he would walk up to the corner and grab a coffee from Jake at Kartel Espresso. Jake stood out in Cabarita. His full arm tattoos momentarily distracted your eyes from his nose and ear rings, but he made excellent coffee, a real saving grace for Jack and 'the Melbourne coffee connoisseurs' who breezed through on their way to trendy Byron Bay where the lattes and macchiatos flowed more readily. Up until Jake and his crew, the town had been subjected to some substance that resembled and tasted like dishwater dealt out by Donny at the local Black & Gold supermarket. No wonder everybody was leaving and the in crowd kept on driving past. Donny was secretly murdering the place.

A cool sea breeze passed through Jack's two-bedroom suite and he thought about how he would spend the rest of the day with his family in Brisbane. A smile came to his face. It had been a little while since he was able to visit his daughter Melissa at the New Farm Clinic. He liked to do that regularly, but his job sometimes took precedence over him travelling to Brisbane. But today, being Sunday, there should be no reason why he couldn't venture an hour north to catch up with his family for the day. He was looking forward to it.

Jack's mobile phone rang out. The apartment echoed with the sound of 'Mission Impossible,' a ringtone that annoyed many of Jack's peers, an annoyance Jack delighted in giving. He looked down and noticed that Joe Boston-Wright was calling. Jack realised this could only mean one thing. He was needed on another case.

"Morning, Jo. How are you this fine Sunday?" Jack asked with a sense of trepidation. "I take it you're not calling me about my health or offering to buy me breakfast?"

"You're right on both accounts, Jack. We've got a body down here amongst the rocks not far from your place. I think you had better pop down," Jo replied with a crackled voice as the wind off the beach whistled through her phone.

"Why the bloody hell do dead bodies turn up on a person's day of rest, Jo? Can't people do the right thing and die Monday to Friday? I was heading up to Brisbane to see Melissa today. Looks like that's on hold or at least delayed," Jack spat out with a sense of disappointment.

[Jo should say something here before Jack replies with his next statement.]

"All right, all right, I'll be there in 20 minutes or so."

"See you then, Jack" Jo replied, sensing the frustration in her boss's voice and feeling his anguish of not being able to see his family. The job keeps Jo from her family at times and they only live half an hour away on the other side of Bangalow.

Jack jumped into his '67 navy blue Mustang and idled out the driveway of the Seaview Motel, giving a smile and wave to Robin as he ventured off down the main street of Cabarita Beach toward Cabarita Hill. Jack loved to idle and cruise in his Mustang. It had been his dream car since he was a boy, and there was no way he would accept a standard issue Ford from the NSW Police Department, no matter how many air bags they had. Jack loved the look of chrome bumpers, not some Japanese plastic one. The smell of lead wafting in through the driver's window made Jack feel like he was driving a real car, not being confined in the cabin of a Ford being subjected to the scent of potpourri. That's what latte-drinking BMW drivers on their way to Byron experience and that definitely wasn't Jack.

The sound of the V8 throttled under his seat as he passed Donny's supermarket. He honked and gave a wave to the miserable old bastard and then headed up the slight incline of Cabarita Hill. As Jack entered the car park of the Hill, he marveled at spectacular view across the bay to the Pacific Ocean. The waves were dotted with a few surfers enjoying an early morning beach break, something Jack wished he could do better. But he never had the time or patience to learn.

Jack ambled down the wooden staircase that traversed the hill, his knee joints cracking almost as loud as the rickety structure under foot all the way down to the beach. "So, Jo, what have we got?"

"One white male, late 50s. Head bashed in with what we presume is a golf club, which was found lying next to him," Jo replied.

"Hm, that's no ordinary golf club either, Jo. That's a Honma golf club, the Rolls Royce of golf clubs. Each club is precision-made. They cost around $10,000 a set."

"Way out of my budget, Jack. Even if I did play golf."

"Mine too. More like something the Chief Super could afford," Jack replied with a cheeky smile. "Who found the body?"

"A couple of grommets out for an early morning surf. Constable Munro is taking their statements now."

"Any idea of the time of death, darl?" Jack squeezed out between sniffles to Dr. Russell, the attending forensic scientist .

"Sinus playing up, Jack? And I would prefer if you didn't call me darl," Dr. Russell snapped. Her retort was accompanied by a stare of death.

"What does a Detective Sergeant call you at this time of the morning?"

"Dr. will be fine," she replied.

When all Jack did was offer up a wan smile, Dr. Russell continued. "At a guess I would say time of death was somewhere between 10pm and midnight last night, but

I'll know more when I've done the autopsy. It's pretty safe to say the golf club is the murder weapon considering the amount of brain matter on the club head. The poor guy was hit with a great deal of force."

Jo held up the victim's business card so Jack could see the name on it. Nick Turner, CEO of Sovran Financial Services.

"Any idea who Sovran is, Jo?" Jack asked.

"They're pretty big, Jack. My sister used them to purchase her home in Bangalow last year. I think they're nationwide."

To read the rest of ***Dead Boss***, please purchase the book from the Amazon links at

www.CTMitchellBooks.com

ABOUT THE AUTHOR

C T Mitchell is an Amazon bestselling author of mystery short reads and novels with a thriller edge. He is multiple 5 star recipient in the 2017 Readers Choice Awards for his novel Murder Secret (formerly published as Breaking Point).

Street educated, Australian-born C T Mitchell has traveled the world in his business dealings as a real estate negotiator encountering many interesting characters; some outright crooks. He brings these experiences as well as a love for mystery thrillers to his writing.

His fast-paced Detective Jack Creek Mysteries weave together traditional police procedural practice, global locations, and a hint of thrillers. Described by readers as "Rebus in a Valentino suit" Jack Creed is the 'hard copper' you want on your case.

Dead Shot #1
Dead Ringer #2
Dead Wrong #3
Dead Boss #4

Dead Stakes #5
Dead Lucky #6
Dead Silence #7

Murder Secret #8

C T Mitchell also writes cozy mysteries.

Lady Margaret Turnbull, the 50 something, widow, is the bane of Detective Tom Sullivan's life, but usually solves his cases. He's secretly appreciative.

Murder at the Fete #1
Murder in the Village #2
Murder in the Cemetery #3
Murder in the Valley #4
Murder at the Manor #5
Murder Shot #6

Two more cozy mystery series featuring Kate Mackenzie's Sugar N Spice Cupcake Company and Selena Sharma Mysteries are also on Amazon.

C T Mitchell splits his time in both Brisbane and Cabarita Beach - a sleepy seaside village in northern NSW, Australia - the home of his award winning books. To grab two free mystery bestsellers, please visit www.CTMitchellBooks.com, or follow him on Facebook or Twitter.

BONUS 2

Here's an extract from Murder at the Fete; a Lady Margaret Turnbull cozy mystery.

.......She and her husband had visited friends in Bangalow two decades ago on the way back from a business trip, and she'd always wanted to come back and settle down. When her husband passed away, that's just what she did. Admittedly, she still stood out a little with her thick British accent, and occasionally people would be brave enough to tell her that her voice and the way she carried herself made her seem a little pretentious. But those who know her realize nothing could be further from the truth.

Eventually, though, she didn't let it bother her. Maggie, or Lady Margaret Turnbull as she was properly called, could have moved anywhere in the world when her husband passed of a heart attack, but she settled in New South Wales for the latter part of her life. The late Mr. Turnbull, a dot com millionaire, sold his email service to British Telecom for 157m pound, leaving Maggie to do as she pleased.

As she pleased, it turns out, was a newfound passion for cooking and eating healthy foods as a way to stave off poor health. She loved it so much that she was eventually inspired to teach others. She purchased Lawler's Loft, an architecturally designed hilltop acreage home with old world charm and commanding views across the valley to the mountains in the west and Pacific Ocean to the east. Shortly after making her purchase, she decided to teach others to live a healthy lifestyle, and the town's bed and breakfast became synonymous with the beloved busybody, Maggie Turnbull. But Maggie was not your stereotyped, doddering fool type. Quite the opposite, in fact.

Running the bed and breakfast, teaching her patrons to cook wholesome food for their own wellbeing, and igniting a passion for food in others provided most of her satisfaction in life, but everyone needs an extra hobby; at least in the mind of a busy Maggie Turnbull.

In her spare time, her favorite thing to do was to irritate Detective Inspector Tom Sullivan, albeit not intentionally. It wasn't her fault she had such a knack for knowing other people's business before he did. Maybe it was just women's intuition? Although the high academic marks she'd received all her life would suggest her brain was simply superior to his, which always made her grin.

As much as he tried to like her, it really did bother him to constantly be chasing her hunches. No matter how much Tom tried to do things by the book, he couldn't ever figure out a way to beat Maggie to solving the crime. Tom's discomfort was evident particularly around Maggie, often getting a twitch in his eye. And that could be seen by all and sundry, something the locals would pick up on.

And she was the only person who drove him batty, even though he was highly thought of all over Bangalow. He did his job exceptionally well, which Maggie actually respected. The man had a real passion for justice after witnessing a hit and run when he was in high school. Tom's best friend was killed, and it triggered something in him that took precedence over what he thought would be a future as a fisherman like his father. As it turned out, fishing was how he spent his downtime. He had the uncanny knack to balance work and family life, which so many people lacked, and was well-known in town for being a great family man. He spent almost as much time with his family as he did with his work, and in his moments alone, took to the outdoors for solace. Maggie always imagined he spent his off days fishing and contemplating revenge for her spoiling his arrests.

Once, when he was certain he'd caught the killer of Julie Duncan, a primary school-aged girl, it was Maggie's eye for detail that nailed what seemed like a random passerby as her actual killer. Tom never would have even suspected, in spite of his thorough yet traditional investigation. Once again Tom's inner anxiety was heightened, but at least this time he could hide it from prying eyes.

"Morning!" Melissa Shepherd, the baker's daughter sang as she waltzed through the doors of the bed and breakfast. She was here to do two things: break Maggie's train of thought and deliver the morning's pastries. Guests at Lawler's Loft looked forwarded to their early morning croissants and Danish pastries, something the guesthouse had become known for with travelers who were food connoisseurs.

Maggie smiled and threw her arms around her, as she did everyone who walked through the doors. Maggie may be a Lady in title, but she was no stuffy aristocrat. Rather, she was a warm and endearing person that people naturally gravitated toward. "Morning, dear! You know where they go." She pointed toward the kitchen and followed Melissa through the foyer. "How's Constable Greenaway?"

Everyone knew Daniel Greenaway, the town constable, was in love with Melissa. And why shouldn't he be? She was as sweet as they came, very pretty in a plain sort of way, and as quiet as a mouse, which was perhaps self-imposed, as Melissa, born and bred in the district, had never ventured far from its borders and was not aware of the worldly delights that lay beyond. It embarrassed Melissa when Maggie mentioned his name. The poor girl was smitten with the constable, but was too naïve to really think he fancied her back, and Maggie teased her endlessly about it.

"I'm sure he's fine," she answered, her cheeks reddening as she hurried to the kitchen. "He came by the bakery this morning and looked well enough."

"I'm sure he did, dear." Maggie pulled the dish towel from her shoulder and popped Melissa with it. As a woman who had her fair share of male suitors of the years, Maggie knew that Constable Greenaway had more than strawberry tarts on his mind whenever he visited the bakery.

If she was any good at setting people up, she would make it her hobby to get them together. They'd be perfect for each other, as the constable was also a quiet sort of fellow. He didn't speak unless he was spoken to, and was generally revered as a vanilla kind of gentleman. He wasn't much to look at, Maggie thought, but when he was around Melissa, his eyes lit up like a schoolboy in a candy shop and it was adorable.

*****

"Are you going to the charity fete?" Melissa asked, changing the subject.

"Well, what else will there be to do in this town next Saturday, dear? Of course I'm going. I'll bet the constable will be there, too," she teased.

"All right, all right! That's enough out of you. What are you, my grandmother?"

"Is your father ready to become mildly rich with that prize money?" Maggie knew when to change the subject, and it made her giddy thinking that old man Shepherd would finally be acknowledged for his wares. The man knew his way around the kitchen better than any female Maggie had ever met, and she'd been all over the world. No one, however, held a candle to Jack Shepherd's scones and tarts, and he made one hell of a flat white sponge as well. Maggie could spend all day, every day in his bakery if she were of the mind to gain an extra few pounds a week. But being in her early fifties, Maggie knew that putting on those pounds was far easier than taking them off. She cut a trim, toned figure for a woman of her vintage, which did not go unnoticed by quite a few of the town's male folk, single or married.

Melissa laughed and nodded her head. For a shy girl, she knew her father had more talent than most and was fairly confident he'd win every category. There was to be a purse of five hundred dollars for the best strawberry sponge cake, two hundred dollars for the best English scones, and one hundred dollars for the best fruit tart.

"Who's the weird old fella that's putting it on, again? I can never remember his name," Melissa asked.

"Mr. Stewart, that handsome old Scottish coot with all the money." He obviously appealed to Maggie's eye, albeit he was probably thirty years her senior.

"How'd he get so much money, anyway, Mrs. Turnbull? I don't remember ever having a benefit before he showed up and it's like he can just afford to do anything."

"No one knows, dear. But he doesn't seem terribly strange in a bad way, so no one really cares!" Maggie laughed and imagined Mr. Stewart probably made money as a voice-over actor in secret, what with his thick Scottish accent. It drove the ladies mad and he found great joy in really working it when he was in front of a microphone. Maggie suspected that was why he did things like throw galas and benefit picnics: to fight the boredom of being incredibly wealthy and give the ladies something to fuss over. He probably considered himself to be a bit of a Sean Connery, although Maggie could never see His Majesty's service employing him. Mr. Stewart was not the most athletic man she had ever laid eyes on. She couldn't quite be sure he cared terribly about the Bangalow Boarding School receiving all the benefit money either. The man had never even stepped foot in the town's home for disadvantaged and delinquent children.

*****

For the last four years, the fete has been renowned for its good food, fun rides, and fantastic baking prizes. Everyone in the town loved going, as it gave them something to look forward to every year. All the proceeds from rides and games went to whatever charity or organization Mr. Stewart chose, and the soirée even attracted people from many neighboring villages, like Byron Bay, Clunes and Lismore.

Even though Maggie was not a baker every year she was a guest judge of the baking contest. And every year, she vowed to learn how to bake properly, though her apple pies and the occasional lemon meringue were the extent of her efforts in that regard. Her big dream was to have a famous guest chef run a cooking school at her Lawler's Loft bed and breakfast. Jamie Oliver was her ultimate wish, but she'd settle for some local Australian talent to mesmerize her guests with their culinary skills.

Her nephew, Simon, would be driving into town for the festivities and to spend some time with her. Maggie loved her nephew. He was a fine young man, but she wished he would get his act together quickly and settle down with a nice girl so she could have a little one to bounce on her knee.

That was the only thing she lacked in life: family with little ones running around. She loved when people brought their young children to the bed and breakfast, though it was mostly older couples or couples on vacation without their kids that came to stay. Occasionally, though, there would be five or six little ones running through the halls and racing up the stairs, and Maggie loved it. Simon was her best chance at having young ones around to spoil, and she couldn't quite convince him to settle down.

*****

When Saturday finally arrived, Maggie helped Melissa unload the truck with her father's contest entries. They were there early enough that it was quiet, though everything was set up and ready for enjoying.

The children's rides were set up overnight, the caterers had already set up the restaurant tent and snack bar, and the local carpenter, along with the assistance of several farmers, had set up the stage and judges' table inside the large food tent. Maggie carefully followed Melissa toward the table along the far side of the tent that was labeled Baking Contest Entries, and a young boy held the rope aside for them to pass by without dropping their pies and tarts.

*****

Maggie is quite impressed with the range of pastries and delicacies offered at this particular fete. It seems that the village ladies have outdone themselves this year. Once the judges have awarded the prizes, she'll have already put her name down to purchase six of Mrs. Grant's scones. "Her scones are the best in the county," she tells her nephew, keeping her voice low so as not to offend old man Shepherd, who considers himself this year's champion scone maker. Simon, whose favorite meal is a hamburger and fries, shrugs but smiles at his aunt's delighted face.

"Thank you, dear," Maggie crooned without looking at the young man.

"You're welcome, Auntie."

Maggie spun carefully to see Simon, who had arrived early to spend time with her before the festivities got started.

"You little! Come here and give me a kiss." He leaned toward her, careful not to knock the pie from her hands, and kissed her on the cheek. Maggie walked past him and set the pie on the table, eyeing the other entries. "Wow, they've really outdone themselves, this year. Mrs. Grant's scones are the best in the county. Will you put me down for six of them, sweetie? I'm going to ask Melissa what else she needs."

To read the rest of ***Murder at the Fete***, please buy the book from the Amazon links at

www.CTMitchellBooks.com

BOOK REVIEWS

Before you go, I'd like to say 'thank you' for buying my short read. I'm really chuffed.

You could have picked up hundreds of books off the bookshelf but you chose mine.

So thank you for downloading the book and making your way to the end.

Can I ask a favour of you?

Could you please go to Amazon and leave a positive review. Reviews are the life blood for an author and can easily affect books ales. Your positive words will certainly help my self-publishing efforts continue.

Thank you once again. I appreciate your patronage.

Free Downloads

To build your C T Mitchell library, subscribe to my newsletter and download your 2nd FREE book. I'll even throw in a bonus chapter from *Dead Ringer* if you do it today. Unsubscribe anytime.

www.FreeCrimeBooks.com

Printed in Great Britain
by Amazon